Kitty's Magic

Shadow the Lonely Cat

The Kitty's Magic series

Misty the Scared Kitten
Shadow the Lonely Cat

Coming soon

Ruby the Runaway Kitten
Star the Little Farm Cat

Kitty's magic

Shadow the Lonely Cat

Ella Moonheart

illustrated by Lindsay Dale

BLOOMSBURY

NEW YORK LONDON OXFORD NEW DELHI SYDNEY

First published in Great Britain in August 2016 by Bloomsbury Publishing Plc
Published in the United States of America in February 2018
by Bloomsbury Children's Books
www.bloomsbury.com

Bloomsbury is a registered trademark of Bloomsbury Publishing Plc

For information about permission to reproduce selections from this book, write to
Permissions, Bloomsbury Children's Books, 1385 Broadway, New York, New York 10018
Bloomsbury books may be purchased for business or promotional use. For information on bulk
purchases please contact Macmillan Corporate and Premium Sales Department at
specialmarkets@macmillan.com

Library of Congress Cataloging-in-Publication Data
Names: Moonheart, Ella, author.
Title: Shadow the lonely cat / by Ella Moonheart.
Description: New York : Bloomsbury, 2018. | Series: Kitty's magic ; 2
Summary: As Guardian of the Cat Council, eight-year-old Kitty, in her
cat form, tries to help Shadow, a cat that recently became unsociable.
Identifiers: LCCN 2017021037 (print) | LCCN 2017037338 (e-book)
ISBN 978-1-68119-387-8 (paperback) • ISBN 978-1-68119-609-1 (hardcover)
ISBN 978-1-68119-388-5 (e-book)
Subjects: | CYAC: Cats—Fiction. | Shapeshifting—Fiction. | Magic—Fiction. |
Grandmothers—Fiction. | Japanese—England—Fiction. | England—Fiction.
Classification: LCC PZ7.1.M654 Sh 2018 (print) | LCC PZ7.1.M654 (e-book)
DDC[E]—dc23
LC record available at https://lccn.loc.gov/2017021037

Typeset by RefineCatch Limited, Bungay, Suffolk
Printed and bound in the U.S.A. by Berryville Graphics Inc., Berryville, Virginia
2 4 6 8 10 9 7 5 3 1 (paperback)
2 4 6 8 10 9 7 5 3 1 (hardcover)

All papers used by Bloomsbury Publishing, Inc., are natural, recyclable products
made from wood grown in well-managed forests. The manufacturing processes
conform to the environmental regulations of the country of origin.

Kitty's Magic

Shadow the Lonely Cat

Chapter 1

Kitty Kimura rushed out of the school gates with her best friend, Jenny. "Grandma said she'll be picking us up today," called Kitty. "Look, there she is!"

Kitty's grandmother was waiting for the girls with a smile on her face. Grandma was Japanese and, like her eight-year-old granddaughter, she had dark-colored eyes and shiny black hair—but Grandma's bob had a pure white streak running through it. She lived with Kitty and her parents, who ran a special shop selling Japanese gifts. It was Grandma who had given Kitty her nickname. Kitty's *real* name was Koemi, but hardly anybody called her that.

"Hello, girls!" Grandma said. "How was school today?"

As they walked home, Kitty and Jenny told Grandma their news.

"Our teacher, Ms. Brookes, says we're starting a special project soon, where we do something to help the community," Kitty explained. "Every year her class does something different. Last year they picked up litter in the park."

"We all have to think of ideas and give them to Ms. Brookes," added Jenny. "Then she'll pick the best one."

"I'm sure you girls will think of something," Grandma told them.

"Kitty, why don't you come over to my house this week?" Jenny said. "We could try to think of an idea then, and play with Misty!" Misty was Jenny's cat, a pretty silver tabby with blue eyes.

"Good idea!" Kitty told her friend, grinning.

Jenny continued chatting excitedly, describing how cute it was when Misty leaped at the point of light from the new laser pen she'd gotten. But what Jenny didn't realize was that Kitty already knew about it. Someone else had told her the night before: Misty herself!

Kitty had a *very* special secret.

Just a few weeks ago, Kitty had discovered something amazing about herself. She'd always believed she was allergic to cats, but one day Grandma had given her an unusual present: a beautiful necklace with a silver pendant engraved with a picture of a cat on the front and some mysterious words on the back.

That night, Kitty had gone to a sleepover at Jenny's house. When Jenny was fast asleep, with Misty curled up close by, Kitty had sneezed an especially powerful sneeze. When she opened her eyes, she was no longer a girl—she had turned into a cat!

Even better, she learned that all cats could talk to each other. Misty had quickly become her very best cat friend, and Kitty was getting to know lots of other cats in town too. She was still getting used to her incredible gift. It turned out that the special words written on her necklace could help Kitty control when she turned into a cat, if she needed to. Kitty knew she had to be careful that nobody else learned about her ability, because if her secret got out the magic would be broken forever.

Kitty and Jenny skipped ahead of Grandma, but as they turned the next corner, Kitty realized her friend was slowing down. "What's wrong?" she asked.

Jenny pointed up ahead of them. "Mrs. Thornton's house is so spooky," she said.

Kitty looked up the path lined with crooked old trees that led up to a big house at the top of a small, steep hill. The yard had a huge tree with twisted branches. It was full of tall, tangled, overgrown weeds, the black paint on the front door was peeling, and three of the windows were cracked. "I know!" Kitty replied, shivering. "My mom says she used to see Mrs. Thornton shopping in town, but no one's seen her around recently. She's really old."

"Some of the kids in our class say she's a witch," added Jenny, eyeing the house nervously. "She has a black cat

called Shadow, and they say he's a witch's cat. Look—he's over there!"

Kitty caught a glimpse of wild dark fur and glinting eyes among the weeds. Shadow was crouched low, and Kitty could only just make him out. She remembered having met him once, but during all the nights she'd spent wandering around town in her cat form, she hadn't bumped into Shadow since.

She tried to call him over, but Shadow turned away, darting through the bushes. Kitty saw the broken cat flap on the front door swinging as he rushed inside. *He obviously wants to stay close to home,* she thought.

After Kitty and Grandma had dropped Jenny off at home and walked along the street to their own house, Kitty decided to ask Grandma if she knew why they hadn't seen Shadow much lately. After all, Grandma was the perfect person to ask about any cat in town—because Kitty wasn't the only human who could turn into a cat. Grandma had the very same gift!

"Grandma, do you know anything about Shadow, the black cat who lives with Mrs. Thornton?" she asked.

Grandma paused. "Shadow?" she said. "Let me think. He used to come to our Cat Council meetings all the time, but recently he's been keeping to himself. He tends to stay in his own house or yard."

The Cat Council was a special

gathering of cats from all over town, which met at night and helped cats with their problems. Kitty and Misty were the newest members of the Cat Council, and Kitty had an extra-special role. She had been chosen to take over from Grandma as the Guardian, the leader of the Council! Kitty was very proud to be the Guardian and had promised to do the best job she could. "So Shadow hasn't always been like this?" she said.

Grandma glanced at Kitty and smiled. "Why are you asking, Kitty?" she said.

Kitty nodded. "There must be a reason for Shadow behaving differently," she said. "Maybe he needs some help?"

Chapter 2

After dinner that evening, Kitty's mom explained that she and Dad were traveling to Chicago the next morning to visit a special fair selling Japanese objects. They were hoping to find some unusual ornaments to stock in their shop.

Mrs. Kimura bent down to give Kitty a goodnight kiss. "Grandma will take you to school and pick you up, okay, sweetheart?"

"Okay!" replied Kitty, trying not to sound too eager. Once her parents had gone to bed, Kitty knew that she would be free to change into a cat without risking being seen. Then she could start finding out what was going on with Shadow and whether she could help.

Kitty waited for her parents' bedroom door to close and then counted to a hundred. Soon everything was still, and she was sure they must have fallen asleep. As quietly as she could, Kitty opened her bedroom window, and then, very quietly, she whispered the words that were also etched onto the back of the pendant on her necklace.

"Human hands to kitten paws,
 Human fingers, kitten claws."

Right away, a strange fizzing, tickling
feeling began. Kitty grinned as it swept
through her feet and legs, then her

tummy and arms, right up to the top of her head and the tips of her fingers. She closed her eyes and waited for the feeling to stop, took a deep breath, and opened her eyes.

Kitty always thought it was funny how much bigger her cozy little bedroom seemed once she was in her cat form. Her bed towered above her, and her animal posters and photographs of Jenny and Misty seemed miles away. She lifted a fuzzy black front leg and giggled to see a small, furry, white-tipped paw with tiny claws. She let out an excited little mew and looked back to see her long furry tail swish behind her. She shook out her whiskers and trotted around the rug on her bedroom floor, thrilled to be back

in her cat form. *This is so amazing*, she thought to herself. *I'm not sure I'll ever get used to it!*

Kitty crouched low against the carpet, then sprang into the air, landing lightly on the windowsill. She caught sight of her reflection in the window: a small black face with neat little ears, bright green eyes, a black nose, and whiskers. Around her neck was a collar with a silver pendant. Kitty's necklace also changed when she became a cat!

She breathed in the amazing mixture of smells from outside: freshly cut grass, flowers, Grandma's herb patch, and the scent of several cats, including Misty's scent and her own. Kitty's sense of smell was much stronger when she turned into a cat—and so was her ability to see in the dark. It was one of the things she loved best about her gift.

With a little wriggle, she crouched low, then used her strong back legs to jump straight out the window. She landed on the kitchen roof, then leaped the rest of the way down into the yard. She trotted through the grass, getting used to working her four furry little legs together, then sprang up onto the roof of her playhouse, then hopped onto the back fence. With her tail arched for extra balance and her claws gripping the wood, she could run along easily. And Kitty knew exactly where she wanted to head first: Shadow's house.

It was dark now, though, and as she neared Mrs. Thornton's house, the path grew very quiet. Although Kitty's sharp eyes could see in the gloom, she still felt a little bit nervous. *I wish I'd asked Misty to come along*, she thought, as her heartbeat started to quicken.

Kitty padded slowly up to the front gate and peered through it. She could just make out the gleam of a pair of eyes and realized that Shadow was crouched on the steps in front of the door. Kitty meowed to say hello. "My name's Kitty," she said, as cheerfully as she could manage. "I think we met at the Cat Council once, but I don't think I've seen you there lately. Is everything all right?"

There was a silence, then Kitty heard a low growl. She had already learned that this was a very unfriendly noise for cats to make, so she hesitated. Should she try again?

"It must be a bit quiet living all the way up here, away from the town

without any other cats to talk to. Maybe if you came out to—" Kitty began, but she jumped as Shadow's growl became a nasty hiss.

"No!" he meowed quickly. "I'm not leaving my yard again."

Kitty frowned. What did that mean? Why was Shadow being so unfriendly? She trotted away from his house a little, not sure what to do. Then Kitty spotted three small scratch marks in a tree trunk close by. They made a triangle shape, and she knew this mark was important. It was the sign that another neighborhood cat had called a meeting of the Cat Council. Someone else might need her help!

Suddenly, in the distance, Kitty heard

several cats meowing a special call out into the night air. They were all voices she recognized as being part of the Cat Council. The meeting was about to start!

"Listen," she said, turning and trotting back the way she came. "I'm going to the Cat Council meeting right now.

Why don't you come along? It's a lovely warm night. You could stretch your legs and——"

"Go away!" said Shadow. "I'm staying right here!"

Kitty decided that for now, it was better not to make Shadow even more upset or angry. She turned and trotted back down the hill, heading in the direction of the woods where the Cat Council always met. *I'll leave Shadow alone for the moment*, she thought. *But hopefully I'll be able to find out what's wrong soon. I just need to figure out a way to get him to talk to me!*

Chapter 3

Kitty ran through the dark wood and headed toward the clearing, where a group of cats were gathering together in a circle. Kitty spotted Tiger, the rather bossy but kind old tomcat who led the Cat Council, perched in between a glamorous British Shorthair called Coco and a friendly gray cat named Smoky. Other cats were still arriving from all directions, meowing hello and trotting to their places.

"Hi, Kitty!" called Misty as Kitty padded up to the circle. Kitty meowed a greeting to everyone and said hello to those nearby, including her friend, by gently bumping heads with them. Then Kitty trotted to her place next to a small black cat with a white patch on her head—Grandma in her cat form!

"I think that's everyone tonight! Let's start by saying the Meow Vow," suggested Tiger.

Together, the cats recited the special words that started every meeting of the Cat Council:

"We promise now,
This solemn vow,

To help somehow,
When you meow."

Tiger nodded once the Vow was finished. "Now, which cat called today's meeting?" he asked, looking round.

A fluffy young tortoiseshell stepped into the circle. Kitty noticed she was walking with a slight limp, placing one paw down on the ground very carefully. "My name is Bella," the cat said to introduce herself.

"Welcome, Bella," replied Tiger. "Do you have a problem to share with us? Kitty here is going to be taking over as our Guardian. She might be able to give you some advice." He gestured with a paw to show Bella where Kitty was sitting.

Kitty nodded at Bella, hoping that she'd be able to help. "Yes! Tell us what the problem is, and I'll definitely do my best," she meowed warmly. She knew how coming to the Cat Council for the first time could make a cat feel nervous and tried her best to make new cats feel at ease. It wasn't so long ago that she'd been new too!

"Well, I'm having problems with my human, Max," Bella explained.

"Is he unkind to you?" asked a little white kitten named Poppy, blinking worriedly.

"No, Max is a lovely human," replied Bella. "But recently, he's been putting these funny white things in my food! They're small and round, a bit like tiny pebbles. They taste funny too. I want to ask you all, how I can avoid eating them?"

Kitty giggled to herself. She knew exactly what the white things must be—medicine! She had watched a show on TV about vets and had seen them doing the exact same thing, hiding pills inside bowls of animals' food.

But the rest of the Council had a very different reaction to Bella's story—and before Kitty could say anything, they were all giving Bella their own suggestions! "You must do everything you can not to eat the pebbles!" announced Tiger loudly. "Hide them under your paws until your human goes away. Then push them under the sofa or the doormat— somewhere he won't notice them!"

"Or you could *pretend* to eat them," added Smoky seriously. "Keep them hidden in your cheek and then spit them out when Max isn't looking."

"Just refuse," said Coco airily. "My human can never force me to do anything I don't want to. She knows I'm the boss in our house! If I were you, Bella, I would simply hiss and spit until your human stops putting the nasty things in your bowl. That ought to do the trick!"

Kitty decided it was time to jump in. "Bella, I think you *should* eat them," she said.

The other cats turned to look at her.

"What do you mean?" asked Bella, puzzled, but Grandma nodded encouragingly at Kitty.

"They're not pebbles, you see. They're medicine," explained Kitty. "Special things to make you better when you're sick. Have you felt bad recently, Bella?"

Bella cocked her head to one side

thoughtfully. "Well, I *do* have a sore paw," she admitted. "I scratched it on a thorn in the garden. It's very painful, and I've been limping ever since!"

"I think Max is giving you medicine to help your paw heal," Kitty told her. "It might not taste very good, but I promise that he wouldn't add it to your food unless you really needed it. You won't have to take it for long—just until your paw feels better."

There was a murmur around the circle, and Bella looked impressed. "Gosh, I had no idea!" she meowed. "Well, I'll give it a try. Thank you."

Grandma gave a proud purr.

"Well done, Kitty!" Misty said. "None of us normal cats would have known that."

"That's right! Because you're human too, you've got all sorts of extra knowledge to help us cats out," added Smoky. "That's what makes you such a good Guardian!"

Kitty purred happily as the rest of

the Council nodded. She always felt happy when she was able to solve a problem for one of her new cat friends.

"Now, does anyone have any other problems they need help with?" asked Tiger, looking around the circle.

Kitty stepped forward. "Actually, I wanted to ask you all about a cat called Shadow," she meowed. "I'm sure lots of you know him, but he hasn't come to a Council meeting for a long time. In fact, he refuses to leave his yard. I want to see if I can get Shadow to tell me what's wrong."

The rest of the Council hesitated. "I don't think there's anything *wrong* with Shadow. He just seems old and grumpy to me," Coco said, licking a paw.

Kitty couldn't argue with that. He did seem a bit moody. "Does anyone know if he's had any problems recently?"

The cats looked at one another, shaking their heads.

"I knew Shadow when we were both kittens, no bigger than young Poppy here," said Pinky, an old Sphynx cat. Kitty always thought Pinky was really interesting, because she was a breed of cat that didn't have any fur! "He used to be a friendly cat," Pinky continued. "He'd play with the leaves in the park with us, he'd help us chase away that nasty fox that used to lurk around the town square . . . But lately he refuses to leave his human's yard."

Kitty frowned. "I wonder what changed?"

"Shadow's scary!" piped up little Poppy, shivering. "I went exploring near his house one day. It's creepy, and he just seems to hide in the dark up there."

Kitty agreed that it was gloomy and overgrown up at Shadow's house. She'd felt a bit nervous there herself. But that didn't mean they shouldn't try to help him, did it?

But the other cats didn't seem to think it was worth it. "I think it's best to leave Shadow alone," Tiger said to the group. "It seems to me that he prefers being by himself."

Soon after that, Tiger announced that the meeting was over. Kitty felt disappointed. Something must have happened to make Shadow change. Even if he didn't want to come out and play with the other cats, surely they should try to get to the bottom of why he was behaving in such an unfriendly way? Kitty was new to being the Guardian, but she was certain that she should try to do something. There was a cat that needed her help!

Chapter 4

The next day, Kitty went to Jenny's house after school. "We can play with Misty and the laser pen!" Jenny said as they dropped their backpacks by the front door. "Let's go and find her."

Misty was curled up in the sunshine on the kitchen windowsill, and she jumped straight down with a happy meow when she saw the girls come in.

Jenny found the laser pen and switched it on, pointing the beam at the wall. Kitty giggled as Misty leaped at it, swiping the tiny circle of light excitedly with her paws. Jenny waved the pen around the kitchen and Misty darted under chairs as she chased the light. "See, she loves it!" exclaimed Jenny.

Kitty grinned, remembering how excited Misty had been when she described the game. When Jenny went to answer the phone in the hallway, Kitty crouched down and whispered to Misty, "That does look like a lot of fun! Sometimes I wish I had my own human to play with when I turn into a cat—then I'd be able to join in games like that too!"

Misty purred in agreement and rubbed her furry head against Kitty's ankles. Kitty knew that Misty could still understand everything she said, like all cats could understand humans. Kitty could only understand Misty's cat sounds when she was a cat herself, though.

As Jenny came back into the kitchen, Kitty quickly stopped talking.

"That was your grandma on the phone! She says your dinner's ready," Jenny explained. "See you at school tomorrow? Maybe we'll come up with a good idea for our community project then. I still haven't thought of anything!"

Kitty ate her spaghetti very quickly—so quickly that Grandma chuckled as she took her last bite. "You're in a hurry tonight, Kitty!" she said, smiling. "I bet I can guess why."

Kitty grinned. "I want to change into a cat again this evening!" she explained. "I thought with Mom and Dad still being away, I could use the chance to go out a bit earlier. Would that be okay?"

"I don't see why not," Grandma told her. "Just be careful while you're out and about."

"I will," promised Kitty, and then she remembered something. "Grandma, I was thinking about Shadow. It seems a shame that nobody at the Cat Council wanted to find out why he won't come out of his yard, don't you think? I know he's grumpy, but maybe he's unhappy. I really want to think of a way to help him."

Grandma smiled at Kitty. "That, my dear, is why you will make such a wonderful Guardian," she said. "You're always looking to help. I'm sure you'll figure out if there's anything you can help him with soon enough." Grandma gave Kitty's hand a squeeze.

Kitty quickly put her plate in the sink and slipped out into the backyard. This was a safe place to change into a cat because it was sheltered from all the neighboring houses by tall trees and bushes. Quietly she spoke the words she needed to change shape and closed her eyes as the bubbling, fizzing feeling swept through her. It was so fantastic, every time!

When she opened her eyes again, every blade of grass around her seemed clearer and greener, and she could hear the sound of a tiny butterfly fluttering its wings right at the other end of the yard. She gave a happy meow and flexed her

tail. She paused to give her white-tipped paws and legs a quick clean, swiping her paws over her quivering whiskers quickly too. She was still getting used to having all that soft, fuzzy black fur!

Kitty's cat ears pricked up as the back door opened behind her, and

Grandma stepped outside. She bent down to give Kitty's head a gentle stroke and tickle the fur on her back.

"Have fun!" Grandma whispered.

Kitty purred happily, then jumped up onto the back fence and trotted along it until she reached the street. It was a lovely spring evening, and Kitty enjoyed being in cat form while it was still a little bit light outside.

As she padded along, past Jenny's house and around the next corner, she caught a glimpse of tortoiseshell fur ahead of her. The cat turned and Kitty realized it was Bella, the young cat who had come to the Cat Council meeting and asked about the little white pills her human was hiding in her food bowl.

"Bella!" meowed Kitty, and the two cats bumped their foreheads together in a friendly greeting.

"I ate my medicine up today, just like you said," Bella told Kitty proudly. "And my sore paw is already feeling a lot better! So I've come out to play! Let's go and see if we can find a mouse to catch!" the little cat suggested eagerly, giving an excited leap and then racing off down the street.

Kitty wasn't sure she liked that idea very much. The thought of it made her tummy feel a bit funny! Even so, she ran after Bella and quickly caught up. As the cats began to trot down the next street, Kitty suddenly felt an odd prickling feeling along her back. Without even

meaning to, she had pricked up her ears and was crouching close to the ground. Bella was doing the same, and letting out a low growl.

What's going on? Kitty wondered, glancing around.

Suddenly she spotted what was making her behave so strangely. Walking down the street from the other direction were a young man and his fierce-looking German Shepherd!

The dog narrowed his mean black eyes as he spotted the cats. He lurched straight forward, pulling hard on his leash, and the man had to struggle to keep hold of the other end. "Nipper, stop it!" he shouted.

The dog took no notice, but opened his mouth and began to bark loudly, revealing a glimpse of sharp white teeth. As he pulled forward, the young man began to stumble and dropped the

leash. Bella let out a frightened hiss and darted away, but Kitty felt frozen to the spot. She stared in horror as the German Shepherd broke free and began thundering down the street, heading straight toward her!

Chapter 5

As the growling dog ran toward Kitty, she finally managed to move her paws again. She turned and raced down the street, darting as quickly as she could past lampposts and parked cars. Behind her, she could hear the German Shepherd barking noisily and the man yelling for him to stop.

I've got to hide! Kitty thought

desperately, picturing those horrible sharp teeth. She took the next left and ran up a steep hill. It was only when she was halfway up it, dodging past tangled weeds and patches of nettles, that she realized she was heading straight toward Mrs. Thornton's house. The cracked dark windows and shabby front door came into view, and as Kitty ducked under the fence, hoping the dog wouldn't be able to squeeze his body through it, she almost ran headfirst into another cat—Shadow! He yowled in surprise.

"What are you doing here again?" he meowed. "And what's all that noise?"

"I'm really sorry, I didn't mean to startle you!" panted Kitty. "But I was running away from—"

Before she could finish, the German Shepherd charged up the hill after Kitty. He growled noisily as he reached the fence and spotted not one, but *two* cats on the other side. He ran from one end of the fence to the other, barking

in frustration as he scrabbled at the wood and searched for a way into the yard.

Shadow hissed, arching his back and tail, and both cats took several quick steps back. Kitty couldn't help trembling in fright.

"That nasty dog's going to wake up

my human with all his barking!" Shadow said anxiously.

"Sorry, Shadow," Kitty whispered. "He just chased me up here. Look, his human's here now. I really hope he can get hold of him!" She'd never run into a dog in her cat form—it was petrifying!

"Nipper!" she heard the young man shout. "Come here! Bad dog! No treats for you tonight!"

As the man tried to grab hold of his dog's leash, the German Shepherd continued to jump against the fence. Suddenly Kitty found herself giving a terrified squeal—the dog had managed to push through one of the wooden posts and leap through the gap into the yard!

"Nipper, no!" shouted the young man, as the dog ran straight for Kitty. She turned and raced toward the nearest tree, pouncing up the trunk, and crouched, shaking, in the highest branches. The German Shepherd tried to jump up after her, but he was much too heavy—so instead, he turned and fixed his gaze on Shadow!

At last, the man managed to grab hold of his dog's leash and wrap it firmly around his hand three times. "Got you!" he said, sounding very relieved. "We're going straight home. Bad dog!" With a jerk on the leash, he led the German Shepherd out of Mrs. Thornton's yard and down the hill.

Kitty felt herself slowly start to

relax. The arch in her back began to drop, and the horrid pricking feeling in her fur started to disappear. She peered down through the leaves from the branch she was perched on. Shadow called up to her. "Kitty, you can come down now!" he meowed. "That horrible dog and his human have gone."

Kitty tried to find her footing to make her way down from the tree, but suddenly she felt unsure. "I-I don't think I can come down, Shadow!" she called. "I've never climbed this high up in a tree before. I think I'm stuck!" She looked down helplessly at the older black cat, starting to feel frightened again.

"It's okay, Kitty," Shadow said, his meow sounding more reassuring now.

"I'll help you climb down. I go up into
that tree all the time!"

Kitty was grateful that Shadow was
there to help her, but she felt bad—as

the Guardian, she had hoped to help *him*!

"Now, you see that branch a little way below you, off to the right?" Shadow asked, sitting under the tree and looking up at Kitty. Kitty nodded, a bit too scared to meow back. "Shuffle backward a bit toward the tree trunk, then jump down onto that branch. I promise, it's nice and strong. Use your tail for balance," Shadow called.

Kitty took a deep breath and then did as he'd explained. She made it!

"Well done, Kitty!" Shadow said. "Now, just one more branch—can you see the one just below you? I left my claw marks on it a long time ago, so that I know which branch to use when I climb down. Jump onto there, and then you'll be able to make the leap down to the ground easily."

"I'm not sure . . ." Kitty began. The ground still seemed so far away.

Shadow let out an encouraging purr. "You can do it!"

Kitty swallowed, then jumped down again onto the branch Shadow had scratched. He was right! Now the ground seemed much closer. With a little meow, she made the next jump and was relieved to feel the grass under her paws again.

"Thank you so much, Shadow!" Kitty said with a relieved purr, bumping heads happily with the older cat without even thinking. Shadow seemed to

hesitate a moment, but then returned
her head bump too.

"That's okay," he said.

Suddenly, an eerie-sounding creak came from behind her. Oh no! Even though things were a bit friendlier with Shadow now, Kitty couldn't help being worried about Mrs. Thornton catching her in the yard. What if she was as scary as the kids at school said? Should she run away? But then, what would Shadow think? They'd only just begun to make friends, and Kitty still wanted to help him if she could. Planting her paws and trying to be brave, Kitty watched as the front door of the spooky old house began to open . . .

Chapter 6

Kitty felt her whiskers tremble nervously. She knew deep down that the spooky rumors about Mrs. Thornton were just silly stories—there was no such thing as a *real* witch, after all. Even so, she was a bit worried.

Kitty held her breath as a frail, shaky voice called out, "Shadow? Shadow, sweetheart!" Then a figure appeared on the front step and peered into the garden. Mrs. Thornton had curly white hair, wore glasses on a long gold chain around her neck, and held a walking stick in front of her. She was surprisingly small and moved very slowly.

"There you are, sweetheart," she said, sounding relieved as Shadow trotted quickly over to her. He purred loudly, rubbing himself against her ankles. Kitty couldn't help feeling happy—and a bit jealous, like she did with Misty—about how much Shadow obviously loved his human. Mrs. Thornton clearly loved Shadow too. She smiled happily and bent down gingerly to scratch the soft fur under his chin, leaning heavily on her walking stick. "You like that, don't you, sweetheart," she said, and Shadow purred even louder, rolling onto his back as Mrs. Thornton laughed. But then she noticed Kitty.

"Oh, who's this?" asked Mrs. Thornton, reaching to put on her glasses and smiling. "You've met another cat, have you, Shadow?"

Kitty stepped forward cautiously.

"It's okay, lovely!" She made kissing noises, and Kitty came closer. Mrs. Thornton bent down to rub Kitty's head too, and Kitty gave a happy purr of her own. "What a sweet little thing." She looked around the yard. "I thought I heard barking out here," she said. "I hope you two are all right. It's nice that you have a new friend, Shadow. I can't

remember the last time someone came to visit."

She straightened up from stroking Kitty and looked around with a sad expression on her face. "Maybe it's for the best. I'm rather embarrassed at how untidy my yard looks. It wasn't always like this, full of horrid weeds and brambles, was it? You used to lie out in the sun while I worked, didn't you, sweetheart?"

Shadow wound around her ankles again as she spoke. Kitty could tell he was hoping to cheer her up, but Mrs. Thornton sighed and finally murmured, "I just can't manage it since I fell and hurt my leg."

She smiled down at Shadow. "Never

mind, eh? I'm going back inside,
darling," Mrs. Thornton said, and then
turned back to Kitty. "You're welcome
back whenever you like, little one!"

Kitty purred again. She was no longer afraid of Mrs. Thornton's house. Now that she had met the old lady and seen how friendly she really was, it didn't feel spooky anymore. But she knew she had to get home, or Grandma would start to worry. Mrs. Thornton went inside, leaving Shadow and Kitty alone in the garden.

"Your human is so lovely!" Kitty meowed happily to Shadow.

"She's the best," Shadow agreed shyly. "I've been very worried about her lately. I haven't wanted to leave her alone since she had her fall, even though I've been so lonely here without any cats to play with."

Kitty saw how sad Shadow was. "Let

me help you!" she said. "I'm the Guardian now and I'm sure——"

"There's nothing you can do," Shadow interrupted gloomily before disappearing into the house, his tail drooping sadly behind him.

With Shadow gone, Kitty made her way home quickly.

When Kitty trotted into the living room, Grandma was sipping a cup of green tea and reading a book. She looked up with a smile. "Hello there, Kitty cat!"

Kitty meowed the words to change back into her human form, knowing it was okay to do it in front of Grandma.

"Kitten paws to human toes,
Kitten whiskers, human nose."

She closed her eyes as the tingling

sensation swept over her furry body, and soon enough, she was looking down at her two hands, two feet, and the summer dress she'd been wearing that day!

She turned to Grandma quickly. "Guess what? I met Shadow, and Mrs. Thornton!"

She explained what she'd learned about the old lady's hurt leg. "I saw how much Shadow loves his human. I think he won't leave the house or garden because he's afraid she'll be left by herself and have another fall, but that just means he's lonely up there too." She finished, "I want to call another Cat Council for tomorrow evening. There has to be a way for us to help Shadow, *and* Mrs. Thornton."

Grandma smiled. "I think that's a very good idea, Kitty," she said. "I'm very proud of you. You're proving to be such a good Guardian already!"

Before Kitty went to bed, she quickly changed back into her cat form and slipped out onto the main street again. She padded up to a fence post and used her claws to scratch the special triangle symbol into the wood, then rubbed her fur against it. She gave a loud meow, so that any cats nearby would hear. Now the message would start to spread, and soon the rest of the cats in town would know that a meeting had been called for tomorrow night!

The next night Kitty waited until her parents were fast asleep before excitedly turning into her cat form. She leapt through the open bathroom window this time and landed with a soft thud on the roof of her parents' car. She trotted quickly along the street in the direction of the woods for the Cat Council meeting. Kitty couldn't wait to tell the other cats what she'd learned. Once everyone understood why Shadow had been behaving so strangely, she was sure they'd want to help him.

Soon Kitty was at the clearing, where the other cats of the Council were starting to gather. Once everyone was sitting in their places, and Tiger had led the cats in reciting the Meow Vow, he nodded at Kitty.

Kitty padded right into the middle of the circle. "Thank you all for coming," she meowed. "I wanted to tell you all that I found out why Shadow has been acting so oddly recently."

The other cats' ears pricked up

with curiosity as Kitty explained about Mrs. Thornton's fall. "Shadow and Mrs. Thornton love each other very much," she told them. "Shadow's not really unfriendly—he just doesn't want to leave his yard because he wants to stay at home to protect his human."

Around the circle, many furry heads were nodding. "I can understand that!" purred a fluffy gray Persian with a sparkly collar. "My human looks after me and gives me cuddles every day. I would want to look after her too, if she was in trouble."

Some of the other cats began to look at one another guiltily.

"I think because I don't have a human of my own, it took me a while to realize it," Kitty said. "Shadow is a little bit grumpy, but he's really nice deep down. He's just so worried about keeping Mrs. Thornton company, he's ended up all alone at the top of the hill."

"Oh dear," said Tiger, shaking his furry head. "I suppose we might have had the wrong impression about Shadow after all. Maybe we should have tried harder to find out what was wrong."

Pinky curled her skinny, long tail around her, and Kitty could tell she felt bad about Shadow too. "Well done for finding out what happened, Kitty," she meowed. "You're such a good Guardian!"

Grandma led the other cats in meows of agreement.

"But how are we going to help Shadow, Kitty?" asked a plump tabby.

"If Shadow doesn't want to leave his yard to come to us," said Kitty, "then we'll go to him! We're going to pay him a visit, right now."

A ripple of surprise went through the circle. "To that scary house?" asked Poppy nervously, her blue eyes very wide.

"Don't worry. You'll see when we get there that it's not that scary at all!" Kitty reassured her. "Come on— everyone follow me."

If any human had happened to glance out of their window that night, they would have seen an unusual sight: a long line of cats marching one by one down the street! Kitty led them up the

hill and into Mrs. Thornton's tangled yard. "Shadow?" she meowed. "It's me—Kitty! And I've brought lots of friends with me!"

At first, Shadow was a little startled by how many cats were strolling through his yard—but as they said hello, he began to bump heads with them, timidly at first, then growing more confident.

"This is fantastic!" he meowed to Kitty, purring happily as he watched some of the cats begin to chase after insects and play-fight with one another.

Kitty and Misty decided to start a game of hide-and-seek, and Shadow quickly showed them all how many fun places there were to hide in the wild, overgrown yard.

"I've missed playing!" he meowed cheerfully. "I've been so worried about my human that I just haven't felt like it."

Kitty bumped heads with Shadow. "See?" she meowed. "You've got lots of friends here—you don't have to be lonely. Just ask whenever you want someone to play with, okay? Or for anything!"

Shadow purred his agreement. "Thank you, Kitty," he said.

"And we promise not just to assume you want to be by yourself!" Kitty added. "Now we just need to think of a way to help your human too. And I think I've got an idea . . ."

Chapter 7

The next morning, Kitty couldn't wait to get to school. "Why are we rushing, Kitty?" asked her mom, chuckling as Kitty practically sprinted the last few steps into the playground. "Do you have a class you're really excited about?"

"I just need to talk to Jenny. It's important!" explained Kitty, reaching up to kiss her mom goodbye. Then she caught sight of Jenny's blond hair. "Oh look, there she is! See you tonight, Mom!"

Kitty raced over to meet Jenny. "Guess where I was last night!" she said.

Jenny guessed the movies, the swimming pool, and the ice rink before giving up. "I was at that house at the top of the hill—the one belonging to Mrs. Thornton!" explained Kitty.

Jenny stared at her friend. "But *why* would you go up there? It's so spooky!" she replied.

As the bell rang and the girls walked into their classroom together, Kitty told Jenny that she'd gone for a walk

after dinner and noticed a cat stuck
up a tree in Mrs. Thornton's yard. She
had already planned that part of the
story, because she knew she couldn't
tell Jenny the truth—that *she* had been
the cat in the tree in Shadow's

yard—without revealing her secret and losing her magic! "I . . . um . . . got some help getting the cat down," she continued, "and I ended up meeting Mrs. Thornton. She was a *really* nice lady. She seemed lonely, living up there all by herself. And she had a bad fall a few months ago, so that's why her house and yard look so wild and scary. It's because she can't look after them anymore."

"Oh no, that's so sad," said Jenny, pulling a face. "Kitty, I feel awful for saying her house was scary now."

"Well, I've thought of a way we can help her!" Kitty replied. "Remember Ms. Brookes's special project? She said we had to come up with an idea that would help the community. What if our class went and tidied up Mrs. Thornton's yard for her? We could pull up the weeds, sweep up the dead leaves, and plant some lovely new flowers for her. Maybe some of the teachers or parents could mend her broken windows and give her front door a fresh coat of paint. I'm sure she'd love having visitors up there as well."

Jenny's face lit up. "Kitty, that's a brilliant idea!"

"Let's hope Ms. Brookes likes it," replied Kitty. "Come on—let's go and ask her."

One week later, Kitty grinned proudly as she led her class up the hill toward

Mrs. Thornton's house, clutching a tray of daffodil bulbs in one hand and a little trowel in the other.

Ms. Brookes had *loved* Kitty's idea. In fact, she'd liked it so much that she had gone to pay Mrs. Thornton a visit that very same day. Mrs. Thornton had been delighted with Kitty's suggestion, and the next morning, Ms. Brookes had something to tell the class. "We've had some excellent ideas for this year's special community project, but I have chosen the winner!" she had said.

When she had explained what they were going to do, some of Kitty's classmates had seemed a little nervous about visiting the house on the hill, and even frightened, until Kitty had told them all about Mrs. Thornton and how kind she really was. She couldn't wait for them all to meet her themselves.

As she reached the top of the hill, Kitty saw Mrs. Thornton waiting on the steps of her house, and waved. "Hi, Mrs. Thornton! We're here!" she called.

Mrs. Thornton beamed at Kitty. "This is just wonderful!" she said. "I'm so thrilled to see you all. I've baked lots of cookies and cupcakes to keep your strength up, and there's homemade lemonade too."

"Wow, she *is* nice!" Jenny whispered to Kitty, smiling.

Ms. Brookes split the class into groups: one to sweep leaves into piles, one to pull up weeds, and one to plant seeds. Everyone got to work, and Mrs. Thornton walked around carefully to hand out treats and talk to each person.

As Kitty and Jenny scattered their seeds, Kitty felt something soft and warm brush against her ankle.

"Shadow!" she said, bending down to stroke him. Turning quickly to make sure Jenny wouldn't be able to hear her, she leaned a bit closer and whispered, "It's lovely to come back and see you again. And you might see me later on—but I'll be on four paws instead of two feet!" She grinned as

Shadow gave an eager meow and purred. Although she couldn't understand what Shadow was saying, she could tell he was happy.

That night, Kitty returned to Mrs. Thornton's house—just as she'd promised Shadow—but this time she padded lightly up the hill in her cat form, with her tail waving behind her. Grandma ran next to her, and some of her cat friends followed: Misty, Tiger, Ruby, and Bella. Everyone was curious to see what Kitty and her class had done!

"Kitty, it looks wonderful!" purred Grandma as the house and yard came into view. In the moonlight, the neat

rows of flowers, plants, and herbs were clear, and the grass on the lawn was neatly trimmed.

"It looks so different. Not spooky at all!" added Misty.

"My human loves it, and so do I!" piped up a happy voice nearby.

The cats turned to see Shadow—who was sitting *outside* the garden fence! "Shadow, you're not staying inside your house or your yard anymore!" meowed Kitty.

Shadow padded forward to bump foreheads with Kitty and all the other cats. "That's right! I don't need to be worried about my human. She made lots of new friends today. And I've made lots of new friends too!" he added, purring shyly.

Grandma gave Kitty a nudge with her nose. "Well done, Kitty!" she whispered. "I'm so proud of you. Being brave and kind and friendly are all very important parts of being a Guardian, and I can see from how well you've helped Shadow that you're good at all three of those things!"

Kitty purred happily. "Thank you, Grandma," she whispered back. "I love all the things I'm learning about being the Guardian. And most of all? I love, love, *love* being a cat!"

 MEET

Kitty

Kitty is a little girl
who can magically
turn into a cat!
She is the Guardian
of the Cat Council.

Tiger

Tiger is a big, brave
tabby tomcat.
He is leader of the
Cat Council.

Suki

Suki is Kitty's
grandmother.
She can magically
turn into a cat too!

THE CATS

Shadow

Shadow can be very shy with new cats. He is amazing at climbing trees.

Pinky

Pinky is a very rare breed of cat without any hair at all! She is wise and friendly.

Bella

Bella is an excitable kitten! Her coat is made up of many different colors.

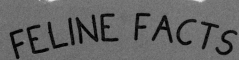

FELINE FACTS

Here are some
fun facts about our
purrrfect animal friends
that you might like
to know...

1.

Cats close their
eyes when they
are **happy**.

2.

Cats can't taste
sweet things.

3.

Every cat's nose
is as unique as a
fingerprint.

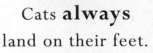

4.

Cats **always**
land on their feet.

5.

Cats can make over
one hundred
different sounds.

Ruby the kitten runs away when
another cat is mean to her.

Can Kitty use her magic to
find her?

Read on for a glimpse of
Kitty's next adventure . . .

"Yes! I'm nearly at the end of level three!" said Kitty Kimura excitedly, pressing the buttons on her game controller. "I just have to jump over this puddle, tiptoe past the dog kennel, and I'm almost home."

"Go on, Kitty!" cried her best friend, Jenny. "I love this part of the game."

"Me too," added their friend Evie. "You're so good at it, Kitty!"

It was spring break, and Kitty and Jenny had been invited to Evie's house for the afternoon. They had made up a dance routine in the backyard, then tried out Evie's glittery felt-tips, all the while playing with Evie's gorgeous new kitten, Ruby. Ruby was only a couple of months old, and she was a very special breed of cat called a Bengal. This meant that her fur was almost golden, with dark spots that made her look like a tiny, adorable leopard. Now the girls were playing an exciting new game called Catventure on Evie's games console, taking turns playing the game and fussing over the kitten.

"How many of your nine lives have you used up, Kitty?" joked Evie.

Kitty giggled as she finished the level and handed her controller over to Jenny. She was eager to get back to playing with Ruby. She bent down to tickle Ruby's soft tummy, grinning as the kitten rolled around happily on the carpet. Evie grabbed the fishing-rod cat toy that they'd been playing with and dangled it over Ruby, who swatted playfully at the little stuffed fish on the end of the line.

But Evie frowned as a high-pitched wail broke out, which they could easily hear even over the noise of the computer game. "Dad!" she yelled. "He's crying again!"

Evie's baby brother, Joe, was strapped

into his bouncy chair near the television. He was just three months old, with big brown eyes and lovely chubby cheeks. Kitty thought he was so sweet. He had been napping when the girls came in, but the music from their game must have woken him up, and now he was crying noisily.

"Come on then, young man!" said Evie's dad cheerfully as he breezed in, unbuckling the straps on the bouncy chair and gently picking Joe up. "Let's go wander around the backyard, shall we, so we don't disturb your big sister and her friends?"

As her dad stepped outside, Evie sighed. "Joe cried for hours last night too," she explained to Kitty and Jenny.

"Mom and Dad and I were all watching a movie together, but we kept having to pause it. In the end it got too late and I had to go to bed without watching the ending. Dad even said he'd make us some popcorn, but he didn't have time. Baby brothers are cute, but they can be so annoying!"

"Definitely!" agreed Jenny, grinning. "Although Barney's a lot of fun, now that he's a bit older."

Kitty smiled. She was an only child, but she'd always wanted a little brother or sister, so secretly she thought Evie was really lucky. Baby Joe *did* need lots of attention, though!

Ding-dong! The doorbell rang, and Kitty heard Evie's mom go to answer it.

"Hello, Mrs. Kimura! Come on in. Kitty's just with the girls in the living room."

"Hi, Grandma!" called Kitty. She gave little Ruby one last tickle and then ran into the hall to give her grandmother a hug. Grandma lived with Kitty and her parents, so Kitty and Grandma were very close. Grandma was from Japan, and she had the same dark eyes and straight, shiny black hair as Kitty— though Grandma's bob had a streak of pure white running through it.

"Hello, my darling," said Grandma. "Have you had a nice afternoon? Mom and Dad are staying late at the shop tonight, so it's going to be just the two of us."

Kitty's parents owned a little shop on Willow Street, just around the corner from their house, which sold all sorts of special Japanese trinkets and objects. They often had to work late or take business trips to Japan, but Kitty didn't mind—it meant she could spend more time with her grandma.

Kitty said goodbye to Jenny and Evie and thanked Evie's mom for having her. She peeped out the kitchen window and waved goodbye to Evie's dad, who was still strolling round the garden with baby Joe nestled in his arms, now fast asleep. Then she and Grandma began to walk home.

"It's such a lovely day. Let's go home through the park, shall we?" suggested Grandma. "I don't know about you, but I'd like to ride on the swings!"

The park was busy with children playing soccer, swinging on the swings, and feeding the ducks at the edge of the park's small pond. Grandma nodded toward a quiet shaded area underneath a row of oak trees nearby. Three cats

were playing in the grass, pouncing on each other and tumbling around. Kitty realized that one of them, a small silver tabby, was Jenny's cat, Misty.

Grandma winked at Kitty. "If you're careful, you can go and play with the cats for a little while before dinner," she whispered.

Kitty looked at Grandma's mysterious expression, then grinned. She understood exactly what Grandma meant. Kitty had a very special secret, and Grandma was the only other person in the world who knew it!

For her whole life, Kitty had loved cats, but she had always thought she was allergic to them. Her nose itched, twitched, and tickled whenever she was anywhere near a cat. Then one day, Grandma had given Kitty a gift: a pretty silver necklace with some strange words engraved on it. That night, Kitty had stayed over at Jenny's house, and she'd had a sneezing fit that she'd thought was because of Misty, Jenny's cat. But to her amazement, something magical had happened. Kitty had turned into a cat!

Grandma had explained to Kitty that her amazing ability had been passed down through the family for years and years. She said that the special necklace's words would help Kitty to change back and forth from human to cat whenever she wanted to. Kitty thought she was the luckiest girl in the world. And over time, she had been getting better at using her magical power. She loved padding around her town after dark in her cat form, when all her human friends were tucked up in bed. She especially loved making friends with the other cats she met, including her very best cat friend, Misty. But Kitty had to be very careful not to let any other humans find out about her special gift. If they did, Grandma had explained that the magic would be lost forever.

Kitty glanced around to make sure that no one in the park was watching. She stepped behind a bush and reached for her necklace. Kitty took a deep breath. Then, very quietly, she muttered the mysterious words on the pendant.

"Human hands to kitten paws,
Human fingers, kitten claws."

As a warm, tingling feeling swept through her fingers and toes, Kitty closed her eyes. Her legs, arms, and belly fizzed as though they were full of thousands of tiny lemonade bubbles. It felt like she was being tickled all over her body.

When the feeling stopped, Kitty opened her eyes. The first thing she noticed was that she could see every tiny detail on the bush in front of her: the pattern on the leaves, the droplets of rain from earlier that day, and even a row of ants scuttling along. She glanced down and instead of her hands she saw two small white, furry paws, with neat little claws, at the end of fuzzy black legs. Her silver necklace had been replaced by a pretty collar with a tiny picture of a girl engraved on it. Kitty was a cat!

Kitty trotted out from behind the bush and ran to join the cats playing under the oak trees. She loved the feeling of the grass beneath her paws and the swish of her tail behind her. When Misty caught sight of Kitty, the little silver tabby let out a happy meow.

"Hi, Kitty! I was hoping you'd come out to play today!"

Kitty bumped heads gently with Misty to say hello. She knew the other cats too: a friendly, fluffy gray named Smoky, and an excited young tortoiseshell called Bella. They all purred a greeting, and another cat appeared by Kitty's side: a small black cat with a patch of pure white fur by one of her ears.

"Suki!" said Bella.

Kitty purred happily. "Hi, Grandma," she meowed, bumping heads with the small black cat. Kitty wasn't the only human with the special ability to turn into a cat—her grandma could do it too! Kitty still found it incredible—and, of course, it meant she had another amazing thing in common with her grandmother.

Kitty and her grandma joined in as the cats gathered under a nearby tree, eagerly eyeing the small birds collecting in its branches. They meowed in disappointment as the birds suddenly scattered, flying up into the sky—but they were soon distracted by a game of chase with a couple of butterflies that

were fluttering past. The cats ran after them happily, swatting at them as they danced through the air. Kitty still wasn't sure why chasing after things was so much fun as a cat, but she definitely enjoyed it as much as the others did!

"Oh, look, there's Coco!" meowed Bella breathlessly, nodding toward a cat which was a short distance away. "And who's that kitten with her? I've never seen her before."

Ella Moonheart grew up telling fun and exciting stories to anyone who would listen. Now that she's an author, she's thrilled to be able to tell stories to so many more children with her Kitty's Magic books. Ella loves animals, but cats most of all! She wishes she could turn into one just like Kitty, but she's happy to just play with her pet cat, Nibbles—when she's not writing her books, of course!